Preface

All of these stories are told imagination of a child that always asks "why" but never gets an answer. It is then left to the child's imaginative mind to make up things on their own and to be influenced by that free imagination.

A child's imagination is affected by age. The unbridled, simple mind of a young child is uninhibited. As they grow and interact, they are influenced by outside stimuli and soon they believe things they thought once possible is seen to be impossible. The Child in the stories, telling the stories, is brilliant with no parental guidance or influence. It is an escape from her loneliness with make believe.

Traveling up and down the California Baja in the winter of 2021, I was awakened to that child that aways asking me why? For many years of no response, she's developed answers to things on her own. I was merely the instrument that put that imagination into words on a page. The experiences we had, are all represented in these stories.

If you can get hold of that wide eyed kid, always looking for approval, and ask them to give you an explanation of why something occurs... you may find something new and exciting.

The imagination of a child experiencing and interpreting that encounter, especially one with an unfettered ability to dream, is beyond fantasy. The innocence of a child has so many ways to freely believe, make-believe and fantasize.

This book is about a very special child I know intimately. I took her to the Baja and she experienced things through my eyes and the eyes of looking for the answer to "why?" The answers may surprise you, unless you still possess your child within. Allow us to take you away and make-believe.

THE STORIES

CHAPTER ONE:
A Child's Story

Once upon a time, in a far away land, in a land of magic and whimsy, where dragons flew through the sky. Animals of the forest, rivers and seas all had voices and stories.

One day Otter came upon a small human child. What was a human child doing in the forest? she thought. Otter took the child and ran off to the wise old owl. The owl told Otter that she had the motherly instinct and human children need to play and she should take the child as her own.

One day an evil witch came to the forest and saw the child. A rage came over the witch and she took the child from Otter and began to consume her piece by piece. The animals of the forest, rivers and sea saw what was happening and summoned up all their mental powers and caused the witch to turn to stone. The final words the witch uttered was a curse that would haunt the child for the rest of her life.

None of the animals could come up with a solution and the child was plagued with dreams and hallucinations that would throw her into fits. Finally one day she broke into a hundred pieces and scattered on the ground. The animals were unable to save her and they all mourned the loss of this sweet young innocent child.

A hawk flying overhead saw the pieces and heard the sad thoughts and flew off to the vast desert where he found the elephant. The wise old elephant heard the story and contemplated his answer carefully. What seemed like an eternity passed then elephant spoke up and said one word, "LOVE".

You must all get together and work together with each of your powers and surround this child with all your love. There is strength and great power in love but you must believe with all your heart you can do this. One of you will have to give the ultimate sacrifice of your own life for this child needs a heart. The witch stole her heart and left her filled with echos and torments... horrors no child should endure.

The hawk flew back to the tribe and told them what the elephant had seen in his vision and how they could bring the child back and break the spell. But one of you must give your life to show your love and give your heart to this child. Her heart was stolen by the witch and she will remain tormented without a new loving heart.

Otter stepped up without thought, compelled by her deep love for this child. I have felt the deep sorrow of this child, I have comforted her fears at night and sat with her when she was not well. My heart is already with her. At that point Otter plunged a knife deep into her chest and took out her heart, blessed the child and died.

All the animals of the forest, rivers and seas saw the compassion of the Otter, all put the pieces of the child and the heart of the Otter and formed a tight circle and began to hum.

A whirlwind picked up the pieces and carried them into the sky. The animals continued their vigilance and continued to pour out all the compassion and love they held.

Days later a sleeping child appeared back in the forest as the animals slept. She walked to each and entered their dreams. She told each of them that it was the love and compassion that freed her from this spell. She owed them each her life. The noise and echos, the horrors and nightmares had vanished. In her beat the heart of the Otter and she would learn to nurture herself as Otter did. This would be her promise for the life given.

CHAPTER TWO:
The Child and the Rainbow Paintbrush: Flowers

One night, in the land of whimsy and magic, a small child had the most marvelous dream.

The animals and small creatures of the forest and fields came to her.

The little child listened as they explained, in only language she could understand.

The small birds chirped wildly and the bees buzzed in swarms...even the small snails, ants and geckos had something to say.

It seemed the world was missing something very important and she listened with deep concern that only a child could have.

She promised she would try to find a solution and went searching high and low.

Finally she came to a big tree... it was so tall she couldn't see the top so she began to climb.

She tried not to be afraid as she got higher and higher.

All at once she heard a small voice...it was a spider hanging from her back legs on a silken thread.

"What brings you so high into my tree, young one?" the spider asked.

The child answered, "I am looking for an answer for the small animals and insects of my small forest."

The spider pondered and said to the child, "I know someone who can help, but you must continue to climb up my tree past the clouds and into the heavens."

The child looked up and was frightened but summoned up all her courage, fueled by her love for all her small friends, and with the help of the spider, began to climb higher and higher.

Finally, after a long time climbing, she cleared the clouds and looked around.

The sky above the tree was colorless and blinding.

She could hear the swoosh of a birds wings coming closer and her eyes adjusted in time to see a huge hawk as it landed beside her in the tree.

The spider and the child told the story to the hawk, of her search for something for her friends, the small birds and insects of the forest.

The hawk told the child to climb on its back and she did, without hesitation, and the hawk spread his wings and flew off.

He knew the only one who could solve such a problem and he headed straight up and into the blank sky.

The child felt the power and protection of the hawk and fell to sleep, nestled in his broad neck feathers and dreamed a dream inside her dream.

The hawk came to rest on a tall mountain top, high above the clouds of the world below.

The child slowly was helped down and told to go into the cave that sparkled like a star, so she went off along a rocky trail until she saw it...

A cave so beautiful it sparkled like the night sky full of twinkling stars. The child couldn't believe her eyes.

In the cave sat a small woman on a blanket of white buffalo hide, her eyes twinkled with a loving energy

and her hair was as white as snow. She looked up
softly smiling at the small child.

She walked over and the woman held out her hand
and the child put her tiny hand in hers.

"What a small child to be carrying such a huge burden
for your small animal friends," the woman spoke
in a quiet, even voice. "The love in your heart and
the purity of that love has brought you to me.
I am pleased."

The small child was amazed the woman knew of her
journey and her desire to help the small creatures of
the forest. The child smiled.

The woman told the child to sit beside her and they
would think together. All of a sudden rainbows began
to emanate from the cave walls and circled the two.

The woman took a paintbrush from her cloak and
captured the rainbows. She handed the brush to the child.

Next she waved her hands in the air and the sweetest
smell filled the cave and she reached in her sleeve and
pulled out a jar and captured the sweetness in the bottle
and tightly closed the lid. She handed the jar to the child.

The child looked up at the small woman standing now before her. She reached out and touched her cloak and she spoke in a soft voice, "Take these and go back to the forest and seek out the spider, she has the power to create and will need to instruct you on how to use these to help your tiny friends," and in a burst of golden light she disappeared.

The child looked at the paintbrush and the bottle with wonder and returned to the hawk who quickly took flight.

Returning to the tree top, the small child thanked the hawk and he spread his broad wings and flew into the empty sky.

A small voice woke the child from her dream. Was anything the child remembered real? She put her hand in her bag and there they were, the paintbrush and the jar.

"Oh spider, I am so glad you waited!" said the child.

The child told the spider the dream she thought she had but here were the items the small woman gave to her.

The spider laughed, "Oh small human, you have met The Great Spirit Guru, she is the creator of all things, even you. Allow me to show you how to solve your problem."

And with that, the spider took the paintbrush and thought hard as she used the paintbrush to paint the sky blue and added a few white clouds.

The child watched in wonderment as the emptiness was transformed into a beautiful sky. She took the brush, and following the spiders instruction, thought hard and painted a brilliant sun. She giggled with delight.

The spider then helped the child back to the earth and she wandered back to her small forest.

"I have been to see The Creator of us all," said the child to her small animal friends. "The spider and hawk helped me to find the answer by taking me to her cave."

The small animals, birds and insects circled the child and watched as she took out the paintbrush and thought hard, the answer came to her, like in her dream.

She walked over to a green bush and with the paintbrush, painted a small object on it, then took the jar and poured out some of the sweet smell. She repeated this over and over again on trees, bushes and vines.

The small animals, birds and insects of the forest watched for days and days as the child worked.

She finished late in June, the time of the long, hot days.

The sweet smell of these beautiful things she created fill the air and the bees and birds were instantly drawn to them. Each was filled with nectar for the birds and pollen for the bees.

Other small animals also delighted in this new thing.

One night, all the animals gathered around the small child in celebration and gazed up into the night sky.

The hawk and spider joined in the celebration.

The animals, birds and insects, all fulfilled, asked the child what was this life-giving sweet thing she created?

The child looked to the spider for a creative name...

"I will call it a flower,"
answered the child, after long
deep thought.

CHAPTER THREE:
The Child and the Seagull's Lesson

One day, sitting on the soft sand beach, minding her own business making dribble castles in the sand, a small child saw a seagull trying to open up a big snail shell.

"What are you doing?" kindly asked the little girl.

"The creator has played a trick on us. He's given us these succulent snails... one would feed me and my family. I just can't figure out how to break these tough shells."

The child thought, "I've used sticks and other sharp things." she said.

"Great for you," he squawked, in only the way a seagull can. "You have hands and are strong."

The child thought again.

Hours seemed to pass and the two sat on the edge of the beach and thought hard together.

They stopped the pelican as he flew by, "Do you know how the seagull can enjoy these delicious snails?"

The pelican laughed and explained he ate only fish and dropped down on them from very high in the sky.

Next they stopped the osprey...he explained he also only ate fish and spotted them from high in the sky, then would dive straight into the water. He flew off being of no help to the child or seagull.

Soon an otter came swimming by tangled up in the seaweed and rolling around a couple of rocks.

"Oh Otter of the sea, how do you break open the clams and spiny urchins you enjoy?"

The otter playfully answered, "Why, with rocks of course."

The three of them sat down on a gigantic rock and starring into the sky and at the drifting clouds.

All at once a raven flew by and saw the three.

"What seems to be the problem?" he quizzed the three.

The child explained the raven the seagull's dilemma.

The raven laughed out loud, "That's a simple problem to solve!" as he flew high into the sky with the snail.

The seagull got angry and was about to fly after him when he let go of the snail.

It fell to the rocky shore with a loud crack!

The raven flew back and asked the seagull what he was waiting for.

The four of them went over to where the snail had fallen and there before them...was the snail cracked wide open.

The child giggled.

Between all the birds and the otter, the raven had used a bit from them all.

The seagull gathered up all the snails it could find before the tide came in.

The otter swam deep into the kelp and brought a tasty bunch of clams.

The raven brought an ear of corn.

The child stared with delight at this huge feast.

All her new animal friends shared in the feast and all nestled down and fell fast asleep.

In the morning, the child woke to the otter cradling her in her arms.

The child thanked the otter and wandered back into the woods.

CHAPTER FOUR:
The Child and the Sea Turtle: Luminescence

The sun was beginning to tire of its long day... so it slowly dipped lower in the sky.

A small child awoke, alone in the woods at the edge of a large lagoon.

The sun began to sink below the horizon...

How beautiful, the child thought as

The sky filled with the most wonderful colors...

Pale at first, then growing deeper and more brilliant.

The deep reds and oranges, delighted the child.

She sat down on a smooth branch and began to sing.

The song birds of the sky joined in wishing the sun a good night.

Just then a huge turtle appeared at the edge of the lagoon.

His shell was dark brown with green edges from age.

His face was the color of the dark green sea.

His eyes told stories of ancient oceans and all the miles he'd traveled.

The child went over to turtle and touched his leathery skin.

She could feel the silence and loneliness of his life.

The turtle took his mighty flipper and scooped the child onto his back and lumbered back into the sea.

As they floated he told the child stories of the sky, the stars and the moon.

The child fell fast asleep and dreamed of the things the turtle said.

She dreamed the most marvelous dreams and when she awoke, she couldn't believe her eyes.

The sky had filled with stars, millions and billions of stars as far as she could see.

She then looked deep into the water... at first she couldn't believe her eyes.

The stars, reflecting in the lagoon, seemed to light up as the turtles flipper cut through the water.

She gazed with delight, giggling as the bluish green sparkles lit up the sky reflected in the still water.

Soon the child fell into a trance of swirling luminescence and stars.

The turtle found some seaweed and gently covered the child as she drifted away into the emptiness.

In the morning, the sun greeted the night and dismissed it filling the sky with pinks and purples.

The child awoke from her sleep, nestled in her hammock at the edge of the lagoon.

Her dream had ended and she stretched to greet the day, smiled at the sun and felt thankful for the new day.

CHAPTER FIVE:
The Child and the Whale: Creation of the Ocean

One day, a small child was walking along the beach. She was very sad

So sad, as she walked huge tears fell from her eyes and filled an ocean

The animals of the forest and streams came to see if they could comfort her but they didn't know what to do

So the child turned towards the ocean and began to walk

She walked and walked until the animals of the forest and streams could see her no longer

The child began to see the most wonderful things

There were turtles and fishes, dolphins and whales

She was floating in the ocean

Watching as the colors were illuminated by the sun as it's splintered light entered the ocean

All at once, the child realized she was running out of air

First the turtle came to see what he could do

But he found his flippers couldn't hold her up

The turtle swam off to get help

The child began to feel tired and began to drift off

She was dying and she didn't understand

She tried to breathe but the water filled her lungs

Soon the whale came back with the turtle

They saw the child floating lifeless

They were very sad

The whale drew on his vast knowledge and opened his mouth

He gently scooped up the child and began his journey to the surface

The small child woke up and felt a soft surface in the dark

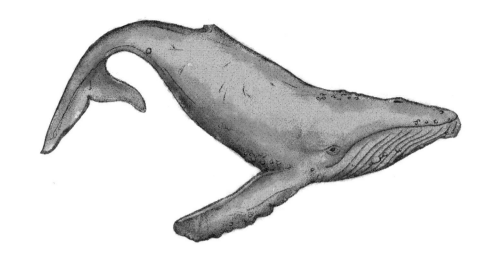

She snuggled up and began to dream

In her dream she was playing in her favorite field of daisies The butterflies tickled her nose

As she looked up in her dream to see the sun The whale opened his mouth

He stuck out his long tongue and watched the small child walk to the beach

She turned around and saw the whale

The animals of the ocean gathered around the whale

There were dolphins and turtles

Whales and fishes

Underwater flying animals with big wings of black and white

There were fishes of all colors and shapes

She giggled as the flying fish performed tricks

The whale softly spoke in whale talk

He thanked the child for creating the ocean with her tears

He told her a secret and the child smiled

Her tears dried and she found peace in her heart.

CHAPTER SIX:
The Child and the Green Buddha

One day while walking alone in the woods a child found a path

In all her days living in the woods and along the streams,

She had never seen this path before

It shimmered with light that sparkled on the horizon

It looked like diamonds hovering in the most bluish green sky she'd ever seen.

She wandered slowly over to the path,

It was the softest thing beneath her feet she'd ever felt

She explored further and further until all at once,

The path opened up onto the most beautiful thing she'd ever seen

Being from the woods she didn't know what this soft powder was

She saw a turtle digging in the sand and asked,

"Mr. Turtle, what is this soft wonderfully warm ground called? It's a wonderful surprise!"

The turtle answered, in a low soft voice, "Why, it is sand, child, have you never been to the sea?"

With glee the child took a deep breath and smelled the most delicious air ever

"I like the smell of the air," said the small child

"It's the smell of the sea, child," said the turtle

The child thought to herself that the sea looked like beautiful patchwork quilt of colors

She thanked the turtle and moved down closer to the sea

She saw a figure standing at the edge and watched as the fish of the sea and the birds of the sky gathered

She walked quietly, not making a single sound

The powdery warm sand beneath her feet brought joy to her heart and she smiled

As she grew closer

The figure turned around

His face was bright like the sun and rainbows danced off his finger tips

The birds of the sky circled him and cried joyous songs

The fish of the sea danced on top of the water

The man handed the girl a stone

It was the most beautiful jade green she had ever seen although it was quite plain.

The man told the girl to hold onto the stone and that any time she needed to be comforted from a bad dream or to dry her tears

She could hold the stone and he would appear in her mind

Clearing away all that she feared and make her know

It's not real

The girl thanked the man and took her pretty jade green rock and went back towards the path

She thanked the birds of the sky and the fish in the sea, turned and walked back into the woods where she lived

She ran back to the Wolf and told him what had happened

When the wolf heard the story he asked the girl to see the rock

As she pulled it from the little pouch that hung around her neck,

It felt quite different and not the same plain rock she was given

She placed it in the palm of her hand and held it out for the Wolf to see

As she opened her hand the rock had turned into a likeness of the man she met

The Wolf knew this man and explained to the little girl about the man who loves all beings

He lives in the woods and the sea, the earth and the sky, and now he lives here

The Wolf touched the girl with his nose

She looked at the beautiful green statue she held in her hand "Does he have a name?" asked the child

"Buddha," answered the Wolf.

CHAPTER SEVEN:
The Child and the White Buffalo:
Bad Dreams

In a land of amazement and wonder...

Once a small child lived among the animals of the sky, streams and deserts.

She sought silence in the vast mountains that surrounded her home.

One night during a fitful dream,

The White Buffalo came to her in dreams
of grief and sorrow,

He'd spread his wings...

Rainbows and fire filled the sky.

In his path he burned
everything evil from the child's
mind and the rainbows were
his promise to guard her dreams
forever.

The heart of Otter still guarded her as well.

With love she thanked the White Buffalo and she drifted off into a deep sleep.

The stars told the story that night.

The moon smiled.

The child dreamed of sunlight bouncing off moonbeams and all her sorrows went away.

She woke to the new day.

She smiled at the sun and

Felt the beating of her heart.

Surrounded by light she danced and sang.

She rested among the flowers.

The tormentors are gone.

She smiled and her smile was brighter than the sun and the animals of the sky, streams and deserts surrounded her and rejoiced.

CHAPTER EIGHT:
The Child and the Coyote: Solar Eclipse

It was a beautiful end to a perfect day.

The animals of the forest, mountains and deserts all settled into their dens for the night.

A small child wandered through the forest, to the edge of the lagoon, and curled up under her favorite palm tree and fell fast asleep.

She dreamed of flowers and butterflies... soft clouds and warm sunshine...

In the morning she woke to the silent lapping of the waves on the shoreline, but something was missing.

The child looked around in darkness.

Where is the sun? Why is it not rising from the lagoon?

The animals of the forest were just as confused.

All the flowers stayed tightly closed, waiting for the sun to rise so they could show off their beautiful colors.

The animals ran around in circles, bumping into trees, and tripping on rocks.

The sky stayed dark.

The small child knew something was terribly wrong.

She sat at the edge of the forest and lagoon, unable to see in the inky blackness.

She called out for anyone who could see to help her.

She peered into the blackness but she heard nothing.

She felt a slight brush against her arm and turned to see the bright eyes of the wise old owl.

"My child," he said, "how can I help?"

"Wise owl... something has happened to the sun," she exclaimed. "My friends are unable to see and we must do something!"

"Let me see what I can do," said the wise old owl and he flew off.

He flew to the den of the mountain lion.

The mountain lion had already seen the situation and the confusion of his family in the forest.

"We need your help to bring back the light to the forest," the owl said.

The mountain lion had dreamed of this day and told the owl of his dream.

"It is the coyote," the mountain lion explained.

"I have seen his game in my dream. He is up to being a trickster again. We must find a way to distract him. He has the moon and covered the sun. This was my dream," the Mountain lion confided.

The owl and the lion used their extraordinary sight in the dark and went to the highest point in the forest.

All the animals listened carefully to the mountain lion.

When he was done speaking the coyote laughed out loud, giving away his hiding place, the trickster was had!

The birds, having special powers to fly in the darkness, honed in on the laughter and flew after the coyote.

The coyote, hearing the birds coming ran away in fear. His power fading as he ran.

All at once the moon began to slide away from the sun and the animals of the forest, streams, oceans and sky rejoiced.

The child was happy her friends could see again.

The owl, mountain lion and child made a plan... everyday the birds would find the coyote, surround him and sing loudly, confusing the coyote so he never again could steal the sun.

CHAPTER NINE:
The Child and the Sleepy Turtle: Mother Nature's Deal

In the not so distant past... maybe when the moon passed into the darkness two times in one cycle of time, the animals of the lands and streams had a feeling of dread.

The Mother Earth and Father Sky had lost a child and they wept and wept.

The sky lamented and huge clouds formed storing the mournful tears and heavy hearts

The animals could no longer see during the day and gathered in fear in the highest peaks as the tears began to rain down in the land.

The child that lived on the beach, at the edge of the forest, saw the rage of the sea as the furry of the clouds made huge waves that thrashed the delicate sand.

The child knew her friends were in danger and ran over the ancient trails to the secret meeting place of the night seers. The night seers could see when the others could not.

They had special powers and summoned the animals and fishes of the sea.

The child was instructed to go to the lagoon and seek the Sleepy Turtle.

It was said the Turtle was the most ancient of all creatures... so ancient that the earth itself had been fooled by its slumber and grown trees and mountains on its very back.

The child knew this journey would take too long and went to find the falcon that lived in the side of the canyon that held the great river of red.

The raven knew the exact place and agreed to help the child. She climbed onto his silky black back, held tight to the scruff of neck feathers and they took off.

The journey took the whole day and most of the night.

In the darkness of night, huge burst of light flashed in the sky and you could hear the very breaking of The Mother's heart.

The sky filled with streaks of light that flashed sometimes more bright than the sun. The heavens broke open and the rains once's again flooded the land.

On the second day, the child arrived in the great canyon of the river.

There was a huge cave in the wall of the ancient exposed rock and the falcon sat waiting. He had heard from the swallows of her arrival.

"How can 1 help, little one?" asked the falcon.

The child told the story of the Sleepy Turtle and that only it could save the lives of the animals of the forest, deserts and streams.

The falcon looked at the sky and knew that there was little time left.

"1 will fly faster than time," said the falcon.

The child was grateful for the eagerness of the falcon to help her friends. She jumped onto the falcons back and he jumped off the cliff and soared so fast the world became a blur.

In less than the blink of an eye, they arrived, but where was the Turtle?

In a dream, the child was given a small pan flute by a native she met. He told her it would help her when she needed a miracle. The child reached into her sleeve and there it was. She pulled out the flute and an enchanting melody shook the land. The earth shook, the sky rumbled and the clouds flashed.

Huge landslides tumbled down and when all was quiet... an eye opened like a giant mirror and the child saw herself but not as she knew herself. She was a beautiful woman with long hair as black and silky as the otters tail.

The eye blinked and more earth fell from the huge figure they were standing on.

The clouds flashed and the rain began again. The last of the trees and rocks fell away as the earth beneath their feet shook violently again.

A sleepy old turtle rose from the land and on its tremendous back was a while world of lush green trees and high top mountains, deserts and valleys, rivers, lakes and streams tumbled down the craggy peaks on its back.

It opened its eye again and spoke softly in the child's mind so only she could hear.

"Your friends are fine."

The child let a single tear fall.

The turtle told the child that a deal had been struck with the elements created by the sorrow of Mother Earth and Father Sky.

The clouds flashed once more and the ground trembled but not a drop of rain fell.

Many, many long years ago, Mother Earth was a small child herself and was cast out by an old witch and her father was never seen again.

She was thrown into the primordial seas and left for dead.

The huge ancient beings with wings tried to save her, the fish of the ancient sea couldn't hold her above the waves and angry wind blown seas.

Finally a giant otter appeared and knew the only creature that could save her and dove deep into the inky Black Sea.

All the fish and flying animals took turns helping the young child to stay afloat. She finally could no longer stay awake and drifted off into a deep dreamless sleep and slid beneath the water.

As the otter rose out of the darkness she brought with her a huge sea turtle that had been asleep on the sea floor for years untold.

It rose to the surface with enough fertile soil to sustain life and the small child. She grew and created a world of beauty. It was grief that has brought this suffering to your friends.

The turtle lumbered off to where the lagoon and forest met. The earth had risen up above the angry waters and her friends had gotten on with their lives as if nothing ever happened.

The child turned to the giant old turtle and put her hand up, the turtle laid his head gentle on her hand and he fell back into his deep, deep slumber.

CHAPTER TEN:
The Child and the Noisy Forest: Cicadas

One morning a child woke from a peaceful dream, the forest was buzzing like nothing she had heard before. She swung her legs over the side of her hammock and looked around.

Everything looked the same...

She took a deep breath, following the air, identifying the smells...nothing different.

She listened as the trees seemed to vibrate and hum a foreign sound.

The animals of the forest and streams became frightened. Squirrel ran to the sleeping place of the human child. Darting here and there, all in a tussle, Squirrel could hear nothing but the insistent buzzing of forest trees. It was driving him mad. "Please make it stop," complained Squirrel to the child.

In the most perfect squirrel talk, the child promised to look into this strange occurrence of sound.

She packed just the right amount of food for a child her size and pulled a wicker pack she made out of a hole in the tree she called 'home.'

She went in search of the black and white Magpie.

As she remembered a dream she had once about a caterpillar that turned into a beautiful flying creature. She remembered the cave paintings in her dreams. Perhaps it is this phenomenon that is causing the sound.

The Magpie appeared with a blue settler jay and they sat high on a perch in a lovely oak tree.

"What can we do for you today child?"

She went in to explain her dream and the buzzing in the trees. None of her friends had heard this sound. "I supposed since you eat in the trees you might know," quizzed the child.

They had seen no caterpillar cocoons and only a strange hollow casing of an alien being, half mantis and half beetle.

The child was puzzled and quarried the two further, "Who else can know the answer to this?"

There is a fable told of a curse placed on an ancient beast. It would devour entire forests in a weeks time, leaving no shade for the baby birds. Huge trees died and grasses were stripped next.

The Jay said that only Mother could answer this question since it was long before their lives. The child thanked them and they flew off.

The child went to her favorite place to sit in quiet meditation. She asked for The Mother's help. A day passed and she dreamed of walking through a canyon playing a flute. Above her was a hawk gliding on the currents. Soon her flute became the cry of the hawk and she saw through its eyes.

Many hundreds of moons ago, a witch came to the land and was made a deal by a prince. The lands were being savaged by an ancient dragon that would consume the fields and forests.

The Animals called in the Witch to slay the ancient dragon. They paid a fair price for the spell and went in with their lives.

The witch found the dragons favorite watering hole and lay in wait. Sometime after the setting of the moon, in the inky blackness of night, the dragon appeared.

The witch had poured a potion into the water and the dragon soon froze in place.

The dragon asked the witch kindly to forgive its hunger and if it could, it would eat much less. The witch smiled and spoke a spell that caused the dragon to remain dormant for up to seventeen years. The dragon was not happy and lashed out and the witch turned it into a small insect, only to come above ground every seventeen years.

The hawk released the child and she heard only her flute again echoing in the canyon.

She woke from this dream and ran quickly to the meeting place by the big lagoon. She explained her talk with the magpie and jay, her dream and the hawk.

The fear slowly faded from everyone's minds. The sound of the creature under such a spell should be enjoyed.

Eventually one day a cold air blew from the North and the buzzing stopped.

Everyone settled in for the coming of the colored leaves.

CHAPTER ELEVEN:
The Child and the Dinosaur Egg:
Geode Crystals

One day while walking along a desert ridge, a small child met up with a lone burro walking in the opposite direction. The burro was dark brown with white circles around his eyes, his shaggy head low and solemn. The child thought to herself, what an interesting animal to be alone out here in the desert.

"What brings you to the desert?" quizzed the child.

The burro slowly raised his shaggy head and gazed deep into the child's eyes.

He told her the story of his life without words. The child saw his sorrow and his joy. She saw him romping around on grassy plains where he ran and played with his family.

The burro told her of how he got separated from his family and ended up walking the desert alone.

The child grabbed the burro around his neck and gave him a big hug and kiss on his nose. "I will be your friend," she promised him.

The burro smiled and lifted his head and thanked the child. "What brings a small child to the desert alone?" asked the burro.

"I am looking for dinosaur eggs," answered the child.

The burro was confused since he'd not seen any dinosaurs. "Are you sure you are in the right place, my child? I have never seen a dinosaur here in the desert, and I have lived here all my life."

"Oh yes," assured the child. "My friends, the prairie dogs, told me of piles of them all over the ground. It is a far distance and I have packed enough food and water for my journey." said the child.

"Perhaps I can help you get to the place, little one," volunteered the burro.

The child thought carefully and agreed it would be faster and nice to have some company. She drew a map in the sand and showed the burro where the eggs were said to be. The burro shook his shaggy head and bended a knee for the child to get onto his back. She grabbed hold of his mane and they trotted off.

It took most of the day to get to the special place. The two looked around and saw no dinosaurs. The child was very saddened that she and the burro came all this way and there were no dinosaurs.

Just then a small lizard darted across the ground. He was turquoise colored with a bright yellow band around his neck. He scampered up onto a rock above the two. He looked with his googlie eyes at the two with a puzzled look.

"Hello Mr. Lizard," the child said politely, "we are on a quest to find dinosaurs so we can get some eggs."

The lizard flicked his tongue a few times and told the child he knew where the dinosaurs were, and agreed to take them.

The lizard darted from rock to rock, shade to shade until they came upon a tall butte. There is where you will find the dinosaurs gesturing to the butte. She and the burro trotted off after thanking the lizard for his information.

They got to the butte by late afternoon and the shadows were growing long. "I will share what food I have," offered the child. The burro raised his head and thanked the child for her kindness. After a fine dinner, the two curled up together and fell fast asleep.

The birds welcomed the sun as it rose from its slumber. The pale light revealed a cave at the base of the butte that was covered in vines and sage brush and seemed a good place to start the search. The burro trampled down all the brush and the two went in.

It was damp and great rock features came down from the ceiling and rose from the floor. The light filtered in and the two looked up and all around the cave. There were ancient bones that had turned to rock all surrounded in beautiful crystals. Whole skeletons of huge prehistoric creatures that were half buried in rock and mud. The girl was feeling defeated when she saw and odd rock sitting on the floor of the cave, the more she looked, the more she saw.

She bent over and picked up one of these odd rocks. It was perfectly round and felt quite heavy. The child gathered as many as she could hold and went outside into the sun. "These must be what the prairie dog saw!" exclaimed the child.

The burro looked at the rock and saw nothing special, just a round rock. He kicked at one of the rocks and it broke open. The child ran over to see what the burro had done. Both stood wide eyed as what they saw was the most beautiful thing ever! Inside the dinosaur egg was the best magic they ever saw. The child remembered the cave in which she found the eggs. She remembered that all around the bones were crystals of every color. "Dinosaurs must've been magic," the child suggested. "These crystals inside the eggs must have happened when the young dinosaurs died in their egg."

The burro shook his shaggy head and agreed.

The child gathered as many eggs in her pack could hold and climbed back on the burro's back. The two rode off into the vast desert in search of more adventures.

CHAPTER TWELVE:
The Child and the Caterpillar: Life's Journey

One bright morning, the brightest morning in some time, the Child woke up from a night of playful dreams. She wiped her eyes and sat up stretching into the brilliant sunlight.

What a wonderful day, thought the child.

She looked around the forest at the edge of the sea and something colorful caught her eye.

She stood up from her hammock and wandered over to a branch.

Before her was a most curious thing... not quite animal and not quite bug.

It was bright green with orange spots that looked like eyes on its one side and long hairs and two beady black orbs on the other.

"Hello and good morning!" announced the Child with a huge toothy smile.

The strange thing stopped its chewing on its leaf and half its body rose up to look the Child in the eye.

As it rose up the Child could see that this creature had hundreds of little legs with little suckers on each.

"Hello young Child, are you here to eat me?" quizzed the creature.

The Child looked in horror at this beautiful creature of the forest and assured him she wasn't planning to eat him.

"Why no... I am mostly curious." assured the Child.

"Why curious? I am not doing anything to harm you. I am just getting ready for my change." replied the creature.

"Change?" The Child looked inquisitively at the creature, still standing upright.

The Child carefully scooped up the creature and ran to the wise Owl.

"Look what I found, eating a leaf on my tree!" and the Child opened her hand.

The creature again stood up, looking the Owl in the eye, and asked again, "Are you going to eat me?"

The wise Owl looked at this small creature, all covered in long hair and hundreds of legs.

"If I ate you, you would not go through the change and become a beautiful being."

The Child was bewildered by what the Owl said to this small creature.

The Owl told the Child to watch over this small creature and be sure it is safe.

The Child slowly closed her hand and ran back to her favorite tree and gently placed this strange creature on a low branch by her hammock.

"I will protect you and you will be my friend," promised the Child. "Do you have a name?"

"I am a Caterpillar," informed the creature. "I am this color and design to stop birds and other animals from eating me."

The Child looked sadly at the Caterpillar and wondered how it would be to live in a world where you were so different no one would want to come near you. Again, the Child gave her word that she would keep him safe.

Days turned into weeks and the Caterpillar continued to spend his days in the Child's favorite tree, eating all the delicious green leaves it could.

One morning, the Child woke up from the most wonderful dream, and found the Caterpillar moving very slow.

"Are you okay?" she asked her new friend.

"I feel strange," said the Caterpillar.

"Are you sick? Should I go get Otter, she can heal anyone!" The Child was deeply concerned about her friend, so she ran as fast as she could to the river where Otter lived. She frantically explained to Otter that her new friend called Caterpillar was sick.

Otter took the Child by the hand and they went back to her favorite tree together.

When they arrived, the Caterpillar was hanging by the branch the Child had left him on.

He was wiggling and wiggling.

"What should I do?" cried the Child to Otter.

Otter took the Child by the hand and told her that this is what Caterpillars do... just watch.

The two watched for hours as their friend spun and spun, covering himself in silky thread until he was gone.

The Child began to cry, but Otter wiped her tears and told her that he is now in a cocoon and her duty to her friend was not over, she still had to keep him safe.

The days turned warmer and warmer, and everyday the Child would wake up to the sun, thank the day for coming, and looked in on her friend. It had been weeks since he had spun himself into a cocoon. His cocoon had gone from bright white to a hard brown color. She wondered if she had done something wrong but continued to do as Otter and Owl told her, and never let the cocoon out of her sight.

One day, while swinging in her hammock, she noticed a crack in the cocoon. She ran through the woods again to the river to find Otter.

The two ran back to the tree. All the animals of the sea, forest, and sky had gathered around the Child's tree.

Otter took the Child's hand and whispered to her to watch, "This is the change he spoke to you about."

Slowly the crack grew bigger and bigger until a wrinkled, winged creature emerged.

The animals and the Child all watched for hours as this creature began to grow wings.

The Child stood in amazement as she watched her friend come out of his cocoon and turn into a beautiful winged creature.

The creature then released itself and floated silently on its new wings over to the Child.

She put her hand in the air and her friend landed on her finger.

"Hello, my dear friend." said the Caterpillar.

The Child looked at this delicate, beautiful creature. On its wings were the same orange eyes she had seen on the Caterpillar, it had only six long skinny legs, instead of the hundreds it once had. Its body was much more slender and its black eyes still remained.

"You are my friend!" screeched the Child in excitement. "How did you perform such magic?"

"I am now Butterfly," spoke the newly emerged insect. "This is what I was born to do."

The Child ran to her secret hollow in the tree and pulled out the paint bucket, brush and jar of smells the old lady in the cave gave her.

"As a re-birthday present, I will paint you your favorite flower and it can smell as sweet as you'd like," offered the Child.

She ran around the forest painting flowers all around her favorite tree for her new friend.

They played games of hide and seek and spent hours in the sun resting together.

After a few days the Butterfly began to slow down and didn't want to play anymore. He said he felt strange again. The Child asked if he was going to change again.

"I am afraid so," answered the Butterfly. "This change is life's own journey."

The Child didn't understand.

Soon Otter and the wise old Owl appeared.

"My friend is sick and is going to change again," cried the Child, and big tears ran down her face. "He said he's on life's journey."

Otter and the Owl sat next to the Child as she watched her friend fall asleep on one of the beautiful flowers she had given him for his re-birthday. He didn't move for a long time as the three comforted him. His journey had ended.

The Child cried for days and Otter sat with her.

"We all will die, and our life's journey will end much like your friend," said Otter trying to explain life to the Child. "We must live our lives as good souls and take care of our land and love each other for as long as we can."

The Child looked at Otter with her big innocent eyes full of tears. Otter wiped away her tears and the two went to sleep in her hammock.

CHAPTER THIRTEEN:
The Child and the Mountain Sheep

It was an enchanting day and the child woke up feeling quite energized. The nights chill still hung around in the trees and bushes. The child stretched to the sky and sighed. What new things will I encounter today, the child thought.

She picked a few flowers and a ripe apple from her favorite tree, and set off on her walk through the woods. She had made a special request to sit with the wise old owl. She had so many questions, but one, in particular, was of dire importance. She bit into the crisp, tart apple and added a bit of a hurry to her stride.

The sun had peeked above the mountains and the clouds hung tight to the tops. The mountains were ablaze with a patchwork of colors. Bright yellows, crimson reds, intense oranges, all scattered throughout the green of the forever trees. Forever trees never loose their color or shed their coat of leaves. The birds and insects began to buzz about with the warming of the day.

The child passed the otter's den and saw she was busily collecting moss and twigs to insulate her home for the winter. She waved and they exchanged a smile, then set off towards the wise old owl's treehouse.

The day wore on, the sun climbed high in the sky, creating shafts of brilliant light that filtered through the canopy of trees. The child was beginning to tire when suddenly a black and white burro appeared.

"You look like you've been walking forever!" noted the burro.

"Yes, since the sun came up," answered the child.

"Where might those little legs be taking you?" asked the burro.

"I have an audience with the wise old owl. I have many questions I want to ask him. He is the oldest and wisest of all the forest creatures," the child told the burro with delight in her eyes as she spoke.

"I don't have anything too pressing to do today. Would you like a ride to his treehouse?" offered the burro.

"That would be so kind of you!" and the child slipped onto the burro's back and off they went.

The child began to tell the burro all the wonderful things she's learned from her animal friends. She told him of her sorrows and delights and all the things she'd discovered since she came to live at the edge of the forest. How she was special and deeply loved. The burro plodded along slow and quiet, listening with great interest.

After some time, walking quietly, the forest opened up and a huge tree stood in the middle. The most magnificent tree you could imagine. The shafts of light illuminated the tree as if on display. Half way up the tree was a wooden door that led into the enormous trunk. This was the home of the wise old owl.

The child graciously thanked the burro and hugged him tightly. She then began to climb the enormous tree. This posed no problem to the child, she had always climbed trees to get away from her worries, and she was good at it. She climbed and climbed until she stood at the old wooden door. She gently knocked on the door and it slowly opened and the owl flew out without a sound and landed on the branch where the child sat.

"Good day child." spoke the owl in a gentle but powerful voice.

"Good day Mr. Owl," the child said politely. "I have come to ask you so many questions." stated the child. "Otter told me that you would be able to answer them all."

The owl moved closer and put his huge feathered wing around the child and told her to ask away. The child began to speak, each question more involved than the last. The owl was taken back by the curiosity of the child. "And now, for the most important question." stated the child.

"Well my my young one, where do all these queries come from?" asked the owl.

"I dream the most wonderful dreams!" answered the child.

The child went on to explain that she had noticed that when the days grow shorter, and the trees come into their best colorful show, the tall mountains are always covered in clouds. Why?

The owl summoned the hawk and told him to take the child to the tall mountains so she could see for herself. Needing to know, the child climbed onto the hawks back and he began to ride the thermal currents, round and round, until they reached the clouds on the mountain. The hawk found one of the big ram sheep that live on the mountain and deposited the child at his feet.

The ram stood taller than the child but had a kind demeanor and soft brown eyes. His white coat was thick and curly and his horns were curled tight around the sides of his head. He looked frightening and yet so cuddly, the child jumped up and gave him a huge hug.

"What brings you so high into the mountains, my child?" asked the ram.

The child began to tell the ram all about the owl and her questions. She told him that she was told to go to the top of the mountains with the hawk to find the answer to the one question she needed the answer to. She explained how she noticed the clouds were always draped around the peaks when the trees turned colors and the days grew short. The ram sat back and listened intently as the child told him of all the things she had learned, telling him story after story.

When she finally finished, the ram told her to climb onto his back and he would take her to see. She climbed on and held tight to his giant horns and he began to climb, and climb, and climb. The child showed no fear, even though she was terrified, she wanted to be brave. As they came closer to the clouds she could see hundreds of mountain sheep huddled together around a huge lake.

The ram helped her down and took her over to the herd. She noticed that several of the sheep would grab the clouds as they drifted past. Then the rest of the herd would hold it until the cloud relented and dropped all the water they held. The water was collected in the lake at the top of the mountain. The child couldn't believe her eyes as she watched this carefully orchestrated task.

The ram looked at the child and said, "Now you see with your own eyes."

"But why?" asked the child.

The ram began to tell the child about hunters and cars and dangers that lurked for the herd if they descended from the safety of the mountain tops. They needed to figure a way to get water so they asked the great spirit for help. He told her that one night the great spirit appeared to the herd and told them of the plan. From that day forward, mother's never mourned the loss of their ewes and ewes were no longer left without the love of their mother. The child felt the sadness that the ram explained.

"This was a great plan," exclaimed the child in a joyous voice. "Mothers are important," said the child, "and being without one is hard and lonely."

She tried to hide her tears but the old ram felt the sorrow and curled around the child and she fell into a deep sleep. When she awoke, she was lying back in her hammock at the edge of the forest. She threw her legs off the edge and sat still, gazing at the clouds clinging to the mountain tops and smiled.